YOU'RE NOT GOD

That Job Is Taken

SCOTT H. SILVERMAN

CONTENTS

ACKNOWLEDGEMENTS

First and foremost, I want to thank my wife, Michelle. Your love, support, and steady presence have been my foundation through it all.

To my daughters, Jessica and Gracie—you are my light and my reason. Everything I do, I do with you in my heart.

A special thank you to my dear friend, Dr. Houts. Your wisdom and encouragement helped guide this book into being. I am forever grateful.

And to all my friends in the fellowship—thank you for walking beside me on this journey. Your strength, honesty, and shared hope have meant more than words can say.

FOREWORD

Sometimes, the most meaningful lessons we learn come from those who quietly dedicate their lives to helping others.

My husband, Scott, is one of those remarkable individuals.

Scott and I have been married for over 43 years, and what wonderful years they have been. To say he is a great husband would be an understatement; he is an extraordinary person, remarkable in every role he takes on and to everyone around him.

He is the love of my life and my best friend, and together we have raised two amazing daughters. What truly defines Scott is his deep and unwavering commitment to helping others. With more than forty years in recovery, Scott has spent his life helping people through their own tough times. Because he's been there himself, he has a way of connecting that's real, honest, and deeply impactful—it's what makes him so good at what he does. Scott has the knowledge and wherewithal to work with people in crisis, guiding them through some of the darkest moments of their lives with compassion, strength, and wisdom.

Scott has an extraordinary ability to connect with people, to help them face their fears, and walk alongside them through any crisis. His calm presence and grounded perspective have made him a steady force for good in the lives of so many. I regularly meet people who tell me that Scott saved their lives.

This book, *You're Not God, That Job Is Taken*, is a reflection of everything Scott has come to understand through years of experience and service. It is a guide for anyone struggling with a crisis. It reminds us that we are not alone and that asking for help is a sign of strength.

If you are feeling lost, overwhelmed, or unsure of what to do next, this book is for you. You will find clarity and encouragement to help you navigate any challenging journey with compassion, understanding, and hope.

With love,
Michelle

PREFACE

Welcome!

This book is an invitation—an invitation to pause, breathe, and maybe even laugh a little. The title, You're Not God, might sound a bit provocative to some, but trust me, this phrase is a universal truth that affects everyone. Politicians, parents, leaders, soldiers, athlete, celebrities, addicts, agnostics, atheists, and theists—this phrase stands for everyone. No matter who you are, there is always someone or something higher, something bigger than you. Perhaps the hierarchy of a company, the natural order of things, or the simple fact that we humans just can't control everything.

And that's okay.

Hold your horses, this book isn't about religion. It is not about what or who you believe in. The idea of You're Not God is simply acknowledging that none of us have all the answers. As Socrates said, "For I was conscious that I knew practically nothing…"

And more importantly, none of us are in charge of everything all the time. Whether we are running a business, or raising a family, or having personal struggles, in this book we recognize our human limitations and learn to be okay with all of them.

Today we see common sense being tossed aside. The world demands perfection and absolute control but deep down, we all know common sense is still there, just waiting to be rediscovered. Common sense is about making decisions based on what we know, and sometimes, what we feel—It is not complicated. It is as simple as knowing when to stop and ask for help. It is as simple as knowing when to stop and ask for help. You wouldn't keep flying if your airplane's radar broke down in a thick fog, right? You would assess the situation. Sometimes life requires the same approach.

So, how do we embrace our humanity? Through personal stories of us. From real-life situations that you will find scattered in this book. Whether you are a leader, a figuring out parenthood, recovering from past trauma, or simply trying to be a better listener, it is all in here.

I wrote this book to offer tools to help you along the way in life. These tools are practical and, more importantly, human. We often complicate things when sometimes it is as simple as taking a breath, reaching out for help, or choosing patience over perfection. This is what the book is about.

This book isn't here to give you all the answers, of course. In fact, it is actually about embracing the idea that we don't have to have all the answers—that we are not God. Ideas, insights, and moments of reflection from people who, through adversity were reminded of their own mortality and therefore relinquished control over to a higher power, may help you understand that and I hope it will encourage you to look at the world a little differently. To relax into the idea that it's perfectly fine.

So, I invite you to reflect—on yourself, on your life, on your experiences, and your own journey. I hope this book gives you a little more clarity, some peace of mind, and perhaps even a chuckle or two.

We're all in this together.

INTRODUCTION

We all have moments when we feel we have to control everything. From a conversation to the trajectory of our and others' lives. The whole idea of needing to be in control is second nature to most of us. It might not be something that we consciously think about, but it shows up in the way we make our decisions and our interactions. We want to fix things, steer people in the "right" direction. Perhaps we do it simply to avoid feeling helpless ourselves. However, the reality is, none of us are capable or even equipped to handle every situation on our own, and even less so to control others. This book is exactly about that—letting go of that compulsion.

The idea that we need to control, that we know better, and the belief in the depths of our core that everything would be better if only things went our way… this is when we begin believing that we are GOD.

One of the most common human struggles is this need to feel in charge. In charge of ourselves, of others, of the whole world. We fall into this pattern of overestimating our own power, whether as a parent, a leader, or just an everyday person. It's easy to think, "I know what is best," but this is a dangerous trap that we set for ourselves. We begin making decisions on behalf of others under the pretext of the above thinking, and without understanding their unique experiences or needs, we impose our thoughts on them. We start making assumptions and believing that our way is the only way that we slip into what I like to call a **"God complex."**

Now, I don't mean it in the traditional religious sense. This isn't about clinical diagnoses. I'm talking about the metaphorical mindset of control—a way of thinking where one starts to believe they have all the answers, that they know what's best for everyone, and that others should follow their lead without any questions. The first person to use the term "God complex" was Ernest Jones. A God complex is an unshakable belief characterized by consistently inflated feelings of personal ability, privilege, or infallibility. God complex is not a clinical term nor a diagnosable disorder and does not appear in the Diagnostic and Statistical Manual of Mental Disorders (DSM). The recognized diagnostic name for the behaviors associated with a God complex is narcissistic personality disorder (NPD). A God complex may also be associated with mania or a superiority complex.

It is not hard to see why this mindset can be problematic. We've seen it play out throughout history with leaders who overestimated their power and then imposed their own will on others. These leaders always ended with disastrous consequences.

But the truth is, you are not a world leader. Well, you may be, but you don't have to be a world leader to struggle with this. It can show up in the smallest of interactions, like when a parent insists their child follow a certain career path, or when a manager dismisses the input of their team, or when we think our advice is always the right advice.

So why do people start acting like they're all-knowing, as if they alone hold the key to every solution? It usually boils down to one little fragile thing—the need for validation and control. This need tells us we are right, and others are wrong. It convinces us that we don't even need anyone else's input, and it makes us impatient. It's that voice inside that says, "Just do it my way. It will save time." But the irony is, decisions driven by this mindset often take more time in the long run because they create resistance. People naturally push back when they feel controlled or dismissed.

An example that I often quote is when a parent sees their child struggling with schoolwork. Instead of asking the child what they find difficult or looking into new ways to help them, the parent says, "This is how I did it when I was your age, so this is how you should do it." The parent imposes their solution on the child. The problem is that the world has changed, and the solution to the same problem that the child faces may differ entirely from the solution to the same problem faced by parents. Instead of being helpful, the parents insist on using outdated methods only to create frustration, which later leads to resentment. More parental examples can be found in a chapter dedicated to it; for now, this will have to suffice.

We see this play out in leadership as well when someone is new to a role—be it a manager or a team leader—starts making decisions without fully understanding the dynamics that are at play. They may be acting with good intentions, but if they operate in a vacuum or just to prove themselves, they will likely overlook important input from others. This individual or group would then make decisions that don't reflect the needs of the group or organization that they are trying to serve. It's a slippery slope—when you begin to believe that your view is the only correct one.

We see this play out in leadership as well when someone is new to a role—be it a manager or a team leader—starts making decisions without fully understanding the dynamics that are at play. They may be acting with good intentions, but if they operate in a vacuum or just to prove themselves, they will likely overlook important input from others. This individual or group would then make decisions that don't reflect the needs of the group or organization that they are trying to serve. It's a slippery slope—when you begin to believe that your view is the only correct one.

We see this behavior in politics, too, where leaders feel they have earned the right to control after years of struggle and sacrifice, and therefore, their opinion should carry the most weight. The problem, however, is that even the most experienced leaders cannot possibly have all the answers. Social, political, or personal issues require collaboration, openness and an understanding that no one person can know everything. But when someone falls into the trap of the God complex, they lose sight of this. They stop listening, stop considering alternatives, and alienate those around them.

At the heart of this book is a simple answer to this complex: you are not God, and that job is taken. And it is okay. In fact, it's more than okay—it is liberating.

The moment we recognize that we don't have to control everything is the moment we free ourselves from an impossible burden. We let go of the need to control every outcome; we open ourselves to new possibilities, new perspectives, and completely new solutions.

Letting go isn't about giving up or being passive. It is about recognizing that we are all humans, limited in one way or the other, and that is not a bad thing. Acknowledging that we are not without our limitations doesn't mean we are weak; it means we are not God. And in that lies humanity and the opportunity to become better. By letting go of the need to control, we actually become more effective. We learn to trust others, ask questions, seek help when we need it and understand that sometimes the best thing we can do is simply listen. Letting go allows us to shift our focus from outcomes to the processes. Instead of being obsessed with making sure things turn out exactly as we planned, we start focusing on the journey itself. We can pay attention to how we are interacting with others, how we are making decisions, and how we are growing through the process. It is about being present rather than being preoccupied with the need for control.

It all requires a Shift in Mindset: "If You Do What You've Always Done..."

One of my favorite quotes pertaining to this is, "If you do what you've always done, you'll get what you've always gotten." It is a reminder that repeating the same actions will inevitably always lead to the same results. If we want to change our personal lives, our relationships, or our society, we have to be willing to do things differently. This is especially true when letting go of the God complex. If we can just shift our mindset, we open up new avenues for growth.

Take, for example, the issue of homelessness and addiction. For years, the government has been pouring money into shelters and housing to find a solution to this growing problem, yet t persists. Why? Because we have been addressing the symptoms, not the illness. This is symptomatic treatment that we have been doing and we do the same thing over and over, expecting a different result. But simply throwing money at the problem without tackling issues like mental health and addiction doesn't bring any lasting change. It requires rethinking strategies and letting go of the idea that one solution fits all so that we can begin to make real progress.

It is understandable that letting go of control is tough. It requires humility and a willingness to admit that we don't have all the answers. For some, this is an extremely bitter pill to swallow. After all, we have been taught from a young age that we should be in control of every aspect of our lives, and we think it extends to everything else. Even society reinforces this in countless ways: through media, cultural norms, and examples set by leaders and, in this day and age, even celebrities and social media influencers. We hear new definitions of success. We are told that success means being the one in charge, the one calling the shots.

But the truth is, real success often comes from collaboration.

It comes from recognizing that input of others is valuable, and from understanding that we are all in this together.

In my years of work with families, professionals, and leaders, I have had firsthand experience of how it can transform someone who lets go of the need to control. It is as if a weight has been lifted off their shoulders. They begin to see the people around them not as obstacles but as partners in a journey. They start asking questions instead of giving orders. They listen more than they speak. And in doing so, they create an environment where others feel valued and empowered.

My hope for this book is that it helps the reader see their own limitations in a completely new light. I want the readers to see them as opportunities for growth instead of feeling frustrated by the things you can't control. I want the readers to realize that it's okay not to have all the answers and that sometimes the most powerful thing one can do is step back, listen, and let others contribute.

Finally, this isn't about giving up your power but redefining what true power looks like. True power isn't about controlling others or dictating outcomes. It's about fostering environments where everyone feels heard.

It's about recognizing that you are not all-knowing, that job is taken and that is exactly why we need each other.

CHAPTER 01 | THE MYTHS OF CONTROL

Our desire for control is as old as humanity itself. Even in the story of Adam and Eve, there's this urge to reach for what we don't have. We all want things to go our way, to influence the outcomes around us, and to shape our lives according to our plans. Some of us manage to grab a bit of that control, and sometimes, that's when things start to unravel.

In both personal and professional lives, our need for control feels natural, maybe even necessary—control helps us feel safe and reassures us that our efforts will pay off. But this sense of security can become a slippery slope in a world that doesn't play by our rules. So, we need to take a closer look at the myths surrounding our ideas about total control—especially this belief that we can control everything, and that doing so is the key to our success and happiness.

Control. It's a powerful, appealing word, yet it's also a double-edged sword. While having some control over our lives is important, there's a point where it can backfire. When the need for control becomes too intense, it turns into an unhealthy obsession with outcomes, people, or events—an obsession that can drain us and lead to all sorts of misguided actions.

Sometimes, wanting control is perfectly reasonable. A leader or a parent, for instance, wants to guide others for their benefit. But when that **impulse grows into an excessive drive**, it can shift into an obsession—one that often causes more harm than good.

The complex reasons behind our need for control are worth understanding. Think of control-seeking as one part of a continuum of personality traits. Narcissism, sociopathy, obsessiveness, dependency—these traits exist on a spectrum, ranging from minimal presence to overwhelming intensity. Everyone has some degree of these traits, and understanding where we fall on this spectrum can help us take steps toward healthier behaviors. For instance, a moderate desire for control can provide stability and leadership, but at its extreme, it can lead to authoritarianism or manipulation. Recognizing this continuum allows us to address problematic tendencies without resorting to extremes. This idea of a continuum helps us understand why control can manifest differently in each person. For one individual, it might emerge as a perfectionist streak, while for another, it could escalate into outright dominance over others. Rather than labeling these traits as purely good or bad, we can focus on how they influence behavior and relationships. In doing so, we gain insights into ourselves and others.

We've all met someone—or some group—who acts like they've got all the answers. You see them everywhere. It could be the politician lecturing on economics without much understanding, or the doctor who brushes off a patient's concerns, convinced they know exactly what's wrong. Or it might be a parent who insists they know what's best for their child, even as resentment builds. This rigid need to control often gets described as an "authoritarian mindset" or "infallibility complex," where a person clings to the idea that only their perspective is valid, ignoring or dismissing any input that contradicts it.

It's easy to point fingers at the big examples: politicians who speak with absolute certainty, pushing aside the voices of millions. We saw this in full force during the 2024 global elections, with politicians acting as though their viewpoint was the only one that mattered. And when rival parties can't agree on basic truths, let alone solutions, it's clear we're facing a major epidemic of unchecked desire for control.

But this isn't limited to politics. Leaders in every field can fall into the trap of believing they have all the answers. However, painting these individuals as extreme caricatures oversimplifies the issue. Instead, we should explore the nuance behind why people feel compelled to cling to control. The continuum of traits helps explain this nuance: while one leader may lean toward micromanagement due to insecurity, another may dominate decision-making out of a deeply ingrained habit formed by years of unchecked power.

Take teachers who've been in the classroom for decades. Some will dismiss newer teaching methods, insisting their old ways are best, even if the evidence shows otherwise. This drive for unyielding control can make a person rigid and stuck. They focus more on being "right" than on learning, adapting, or listening.

Here's where the continuum becomes even more useful: understanding these behaviors as a spectrum of traits can help us identify how to intervene. A teacher dismissing new methods may not be a lost cause; they might be open to change if approached with evidence and empathy. Similarly, a controlling parent might shift their approach when they realize the emotional toll their behavior takes on their child. The goal is to move slightly along the continuum toward healthier expressions of these tendencies, rather than expecting drastic overnight change.

And what are the consequences of this mindset? They're different in each situation but usually damaging to everyone involved, including the person holding onto control. Think of a doctor who sees patients with a "know-it-all" attitude. When they ignore the patient's experience and concerns, it can lead to misdiagnosis and even harm. Or consider our courtrooms—lawyers and judges hold great power, and when they become detached from the human aspect of their cases, lives can be ruined. A judge who won't look up from a file to engage with the person in front of them is exercising a dangerous level of unchecked control, reducing someone's life to mere paperwork.

When control becomes an obsession, the results are often devastating.

So, why do we cling to control so tightly? Why do people feel the need to dominate every situation, every conversation, and every decision? The answer isn't simple. It comes from a mix of social, psychological, and cultural factors.

On one hand, the desire for control is a natural reaction. We're wired to resist uncertainty—and what's more uncertain than life itself? Life can feel like it's constantly teetering on the edge of chaos, so we impose control on our surroundings to create a sense of stability. That's why people create strict schedules, set goals in stone, and stick to routines—we need to feel in control; it makes us feel secure.

History gives us good examples of finding the right balance when it comes to control. Franklin D. Roosevelt, during World War II, faced enormous pressure to make decisions that would shape the future. Even though he held great power as President, he knew the value of working with others. He relied on his trusted advisors and cabinet members, giving them tasks and listening to their expertise to handle the global crisis. Roosevelt's trust in others made him a stronger leader and allowed his team to respond quickly to the challenges they faced. His leadership wasn't about controlling every detail but about building a team where everyone's ideas were valued.

Similarly, Steve Jobs, known for his strong opinions and perfectionism, understood that he couldn't do everything himself. At Apple, he knew when to step back and let his team take charge, especially on projects where their skills were stronger than his. For example, he trusted his design team to shape groundbreaking products like the iPhone and iPad. By empowering his team, he helped Apple achieve incredible results. Jobs led by inspiring others and setting a clear vision, rather than trying to control every small decision.

Both Roosevelt and Jobs showed how important it is to find a healthy way to use control. They knew that real leadership isn't about making every decision yourself, but about trusting others to contribute and grow. These examples remind us that success often comes from building trust, delegating wisely, and adapting to change. By accepting their own limits and relying on the strengths of others, they left behind legacies that lasted far beyond their time.

These stories show us that letting go of total control isn't a weakness—it's a sign of strength. It takes humility to admit you don't know everything and confidence to trust others with important responsibilities. Leaders like Roosevelt and Jobs prove that letting go of control doesn't mean giving up your authority; it means using it to create an environment where people can thrive, innovate, and grow.

For many, it's also about a personal sense of importance. Some people, driven by a desire to make an impact, may start tuning out others' input or thinking their perspective is better. This behavior, often fueled by insecurity or past experiences, makes them believe that controlling others or situations is the only path to success.

Then there's the influence of learning and habit. Many people learn the need for control from watching others. A child who grows up with controlling parents might adopt similar behaviors, not because they know it's good or bad, but because it's what they know. To them, dominance feels normal and effective. In professional settings, people mimic the behavior of higher-ups, assuming that success means being in control. Over time, they stop seeking feedback, convinced they're the only ones with the right answers.

But the truth is, no one has complete control over all circumstances. Life is way too complex and unpredictable for that. And trying to control everything, beyond a healthy level, leads to stress, burnout, and frustration.

In both personal and professional settings, an obsession with control backfires. These people refuse advice, dismiss feedback, and stubbornly cling to their ideas even when there's clear evidence they're wrong. At work, a manager who ignores their team's input pushes forward with plans that everyone else can see will fail. And in personal life, it might be the parent who insists on making every choice for their child.

When things go wrong, people like this tend to shift the blame or make excuses rather than acknowledge their limits. Over time, this alienates colleagues, friends, and family who get tired of dealing with someone who won't listen, who insists on being in control all the time. Eventually, people like this end up isolated. They cut themselves off from meaningful relationships and helpful feedback, and their personal and professional lives suffer. As those around them grow weary of their behavior, their lives become strained, and their growth stops.

In the end, people who cling too tightly to control often find themselves alone and irrelevant.

But what would happen if we could let go of some of that need for control? What happens when we ease our grip on outcomes and accept things as they are?

When we acknowledge that we don't have all the answers, we open ourselves up to learn, grow, and connect with others. We become better leaders, partners, parents, friends, managers, lawyers, judges, doctors, and ultimately, better people because we're willing to listen, learn, and adapt.

History shows us that some of the most successful people were those who understood the value of letting go of control. They knew that success isn't about controlling every little thing but about navigating life's uncertainties with openness. It's not about overconfidence but about trusting others, inviting their ideas, and being willing to change course. These people achieved far more than they would have through sheer force of will.

That's not to say that letting go of control is easy. Changing this mindset can feel like moving a mountain. It means accepting uncertainty, trusting those around us, and acknowledging we don't know everything. It takes a lot of self-respect, humility, patience, empathy, and a willingness to be vulnerable.

But in the end, letting go of control allows us to live with more peace.

The myths of control are just that—myths. No matter how much we try, we'll never be able to control everything. Life is just too unpredictable, and the more we try to impose our control, the more we close ourselves off to new possibilities, learning, and growth. Understanding that we don't need to control everything is not about surrendering control entirely but about recognizing the limits of control.

Real success isn't about controlling every outcome; it's about enjoying the journey, trusting those who accompany us, and most importantly, trusting the process. Sometimes the best thing we can do is simply listen. That's the essence of an authentic life.

Life isn't fair. It's never going to be fair. Accept it. Let go of the need for absolute control and embrace reality, not as a defeat but as a step toward peace in the middle of the chaos.

CHAPTER 02 | EDGING GOD OUT

Leadership is like juggling—you're constantly balancing power, responsibilities, and expectations. It often feels like an immense responsibility, especially when others are looking to you for guidance and wisdom. History, politics, business, and even our personal lives show us that leadership often crumbles under one persistent, subtle problem: the belief that one is irreplaceable. This idea doesn't just surface in a few sectors; it seeps into every position of authority—from political leaders and CEOs to religious figures, athletes, and parents. Leadership failures often grow from this mentality.

There are often subtle warning signs of arrogance and hubris that go unnoticed even when we're in positions of power. Here, arrogance means an unwillingness to accept input from others—a stubbornness that blinds leaders to feedback and limits their ability to adapt.

Leadership failures don't always stem from incompetence. More often, they come from a leader's refusal to acknowledge their own fallibility. In fact, not being able to accept one's own fallibility could be seen as the greatest form of incompetence.

Incompetence isn't just about lacking skill; it can stem from a refusal to acknowledge limitations—a form of arrogance-driven incompetence. Leaders fail when they see themselves as omniscient and omnipotent, convinced they're beyond error. This mindset creates a culture where feedback is ignored and dissent stifled, leading to small, unchecked mistakes that ultimately spiral into major failures.

In my experience coaching people in positions of power, I've come across leaders who stumble in their roles because they're unable to adapt or respond to feedback. Instead of seeking input or adjusting course, they dig in, pushing stubbornly forward. When leaders are deaf to feedback and unwilling to accept input, their followers grow hesitant to voice concerns. Even a small deviation in direction, if left unchecked, can eventually leave a leader and their team far from their intended destination. The same principle applies to leadership: small, unchecked missteps accumulate until they become devastating.

A glaring example of this is how the COVID-19 pandemic was handled in the United States under President Trump. He frequently assured everyone that "everything will be fine" and downplayed the virus, leading to a delayed response that cost billions and countless lives. This type of leadership—refusing to admit mistakes and resisting expert advice—illustrates how dangerous it is when leaders believe they can't fail. In the end, they end up guiding their team or nation further off course, often with devastating consequences.

Consider, for example, Adam Neumann, the CEO of WeWork, whose refusal to heed advice about the company's unsustainable growth strategy led to the collapse of its IPO and the company's value plummeting. Or think about sports coaches like Bobby Knight, whose rigid and abusive style alienated players and eventually led to his dismissal from

Indiana University. These examples highlight how ignoring input and refusing to adapt can lead to professional and personal failure.

Another common issue, though not always obvious, is arrogance. Arrogant leaders resist input, creating environments where essential feedback is blocked. Arrogance in leadership is not always loud or overt. In fact, it can manifest as what I call "shy arrogance." Shy-arrogant leaders may appear polite and reserved but resist change and block feedback at every opportunity. A refusal to adapt when outcomes diverge from the original plan is a telltale sign. Leaders like these believe they know best, and if they don't agree with the data or outcomes, they resist making necessary changes—ultimately jeopardizing their success.

This kind of behavior is especially common among leaders who, with supreme confidence, defend their actions even as their organization falters. Take some CEOs, for example. In companies, this type of leader often focuses solely on pleasing shareholders or board members, losing sight of the broader needs of their employees and customers. A CEO who had early career success may fixate on gaining approval from a group of influential investors, ignoring feedback from within the company. This, in turn, leads to declining morale and productivity. Often, an external consultant has to be brought in to assess the situation, and although adjustments are made, the damage is often already done.

The danger of arrogance isn't limited to CEOs; it permeates all walks of life and shows up in a variety of roles. In education, for example, a teacher who clings to outdated methods and resists change risks declining student engagement and growth. By refusing to adapt, they stifle creativity and critical thinking, leaving students feeling undervalued and uninspired. When students aren't encouraged to explore and innovate, their enthusiasm for learning diminishes, leading to disengagement.

Similarly, if a sports coach stubbornly refuses to seek out new strategies, they risk stalling their team's growth. Sports evolve with every game, and inflexibility on the part of the coach leads to losses, eroding team morale and undermining trust in the leader. Athletes thrive on growth and development, and if they sense that their coach is closed off to new ideas, their motivation dies.

In family dynamics, parents who don't allow their children to make independent decisions show a form of arrogance that can leave lasting effects on their child's mindset. Parents who insist on controlling every aspect of their child's life, from friendships to academics, undermine the child's decision-making skills. The child misses opportunities to learn from their mistakes and doesn't fully develop cognitive abilities.

The real costs of this arrogance extend beyond individual relationships, rippling out into organizations and communities. Leaders who are inflexible and resist feedback create cultures of disengagement. The antidote to this is humility.

So, what does humility in leadership look like? Simply put, humility is the willingness to admit when you're wrong, to listen to others, and to make changes when necessary. This mindset applies across all areas of life. A parent might realize that being too strict is pushing their child away and choose to create a more supportive environment. A CEO might recognize that a new strategy isn't working and adjust based on employee feedback. And a political leader might acknowledge that their initial plan needs revision and listen to the people or advisors in their constituency.

Humility in leadership isn't about being weak or indecisive; it's about being open to the reality that you don't have all the answers. Allowing the team to shine makes the collective success greater than any one individual's. The ability to reflect, accept feedback, and make changes strengthens both the leader and the entire organization or community they serve.

To remain effective, leaders need two essential practices: self-awareness and constructive action. Self-awareness involves the ability to pause, reflect, and assess when ego or bias is clouding judgment. Constructive action requires decisive steps to address issues, seek feedback, and implement necessary changes. Together, these practices create a balanced approach that keeps leaders grounded and adaptable.

Take, for example, a CEO who struggled to manage the demands of running a large company because they refused to share responsibilities. Over time, they realized that trying to control everything themselves was holding the company back. By delegating key tasks to capable managers and trusting them to lead, the CEO was able to focus on the bigger picture. This change made the company more efficient, boosted team morale, and showed how good leadership often means letting others step up.

Leaders also need to recognize when their pride or overconfidence is causing problems. Ignoring feedback or clinging to failing strategies can hurt both the leader and the organization. A great leader listens to others and isn't afraid to admit when something isn't working so they can make the necessary changes.

An example of this is the conflict between General Douglas MacArthur and President Harry Truman during the Korean War. MacArthur believed he was always right and ignored Truman's orders, leading to his dismissal. This shows how important it is for leaders to understand their limits and respect the authority of others.

Arrogant leaders often attract followers because of their confidence, but this can lead to problems when no one feels comfortable speaking up. Fear and insecurity can stop people from challenging a leader, even when it's clear they're making mistakes.

Good leaders know they can't do everything on their own. They listen to feedback, admit when they're wrong, and encourage teamwork. By doing this, they not only improve as leaders but also create organizations that are stronger, more flexible, and better prepared to handle challenges.

In the end, humility in leadership boils down to one fundamental truth: you are neither omniscient nor omnipotent. No matter how powerful, intelligent, or successful you are, you are human—and fallible. Great leaders understand this. They know when to wield the Hammer of Humility to break through their own or others' egos, and they know when to rest in the Hammock of Humility. The balance between action and reflection, between control and delegation, is what defines great leadership. Whether leading a country, a company, or a family, the ability to admit you don't have all the answers is, ultimately, the answer.

In politics, business, and personal life, leaders who succeed long-term are those who know when to seek help from others. They understand that leadership isn't about being irreplaceable—it's about being adaptable, humble, kind, and wise enough to know when to let go.

CHAPTER 03 | SELF-AWARENESS OF A LISTENER

Listening.

We talk about it all the time, but how often do we really think about what it means?

Most of us assume we're good at it; after all, isn't listening just a matter of paying attention? But true listening is more than just nodding along or waiting for our turn to speak. It's a skill that, when practiced with care, can reveal a lot—not only about the person we're listening to but also about ourselves.

In my experience, listening is one of the most underrated tools we have for building empathy, personal growth, and real connection. It's easy to overlook, but once you start listening deeply, you realize how powerful it can be.

To me, true listening is an act of humility. It means holding back our natural urge to jump in, respond, or fix things. It's about letting go of the need to bring in our own experiences and, instead, allowing someone else's words to simply wash over us. This approach can be just as powerful for us as it is for the person we're listening to. Picture yourself sitting with someone, really hearing not only what they're saying but also the feelings and fears they're not putting into words. When we listen with self-awareness, we create a space for them to be fully themselves, without judgment or interruption—just an honest moment to share their truth.

But here's the thing: it's a lot harder than it sounds. Our biases and assumptions have a way of sneaking in before we even notice. I've seen this again and again as a coach—especially with clients who try to justify their past choices, hoping to steer the conversation in a certain direction. In those moments, my role isn't to simply agree with their story or to push back. It's to listen, to really understand the story they're telling, and to make sure they feel heard. In these situations, listening with self-awareness isn't just a technique; it's a discipline. It allows me to respond with thoughtfulness and without judgment.

The Ego and the Trap of Knowing It All

Self-awareness in listening often boils down to one simple truth: we don't have all the answers. But when people look to us for guidance, it's easy to slip into the "I know best" mindset. This can lead to what I call the "false god complex"—the belief that we're the ones who can fix things for others. Yet, ego doesn't have to be pushed aside entirely; instead, it can adjust to support real listening. Ego is tricky that way; it sneaks in, even when we think we're being open. That's why I practice what I call "active humility"— allow my ego to make room for someone else's perspective, rather than overshadow it, remembering that my role as a listener isn't to confirm my own perspective but to truly understand theirs. Ego, in this sense, isn't something we need to eliminate; it's something we learn to soften and guide, so it serves the process of connection.

I remember a client struggling with addiction who was searching for a lifeline. Instead of jumping in with solutions,

I asked him a simple question: "How's that working for you?" This wasn't a judgment but a prompt for him to pause and consider his own choices. In that moment, he realized, without me telling him, that his way wasn't working. Listening with active humility means helping someone find their own insights, not pushing ours onto them. It's a humbling reminder that, often, the most powerful answers come from within, not from us as coaches or guides. In these moments, my ego isn't absent; it's simply steady and open, willing to make space for the other person's path without imposing my own.

Empathy vs. Sympathy: Two Sides of Listening

Empathy plays a huge role in active listening. Empathy isn't about giving advice or passing judgment—it's about meeting someone where they are, as an equal. It's what makes listening a bridge between two people's perspectives. Unlike sympathy, which can sometimes create distance, empathy brings us closer. It's like holding up a mirror—not just for the person we're listening to but for ourselves, too. When we listen with empathy, we're saying, "Your perspective matters," and that opens us up to reflect on our own biases and vulnerabilities.

I remember a coaching session with someone whose struggles mirrored my own. As he spoke, I felt a deep connection through our shared pain. I understood, on a gut level, where he was coming from. That's the power of empathy—it connects us in ways that advice or sympathy just can't. But true empathy means keeping our own experiences in check. It's not about jumping in to share our pain; it's about holding space for theirs. This difference is essential because, if we're not careful, we might unintentionally make their journey about us.

Techniques for True Listening

Listening with self-awareness isn't something you can just turn on and off—it takes practice. Over time, I've picked up a few simple techniques to help me stay grounded. One of them is as straightforward as it sounds: I close my mouth, focus my attention, and let my client's words fill the space. In these moments, I remind myself that they don't need a lecture or a quick fix; they just need to feel heard. If my mind starts wandering or I feel my own biases creeping in, I ground myself by placing my hands on my thighs. It's a small physical action, but it keeps me focused and helps counter the usual distractions.

Setting boundaries is also essential. In my work, clients often share painful stories of addiction, trauma, or loss, and it's easy to get emotionally wrapped up in their struggles. Setting boundaries doesn't mean shutting them out; it means protecting my own emotional space so I can be fully there for them. My role is to listen, not to fix everything. With clear boundaries, I can empathize without getting overwhelmed, offering support without taking on their struggles as my own. This allows me to listen with both clarity and compassion.

Reflection Through Listening

Every conversation I have, every story I hear, holds up a mirror for me. Listening isn't just about understanding someone else—it's also a way to learn more about ourselves. In one particularly tough session, a client's story hit close to home and stirred up memories I hadn't faced in years. In that moment, I realized I still had some biases and unresolved feelings to work through. These reflections have helped me grow, not just as a coach but as a person. They remind me that, while I'm there to guide, I'm also there to learn.

This kind of deep, reflective listening has shown me my own emotional triggers and hidden biases. It's helped me see where I still have room to grow. Listening without planning a response or jumping in with advice isn't easy, but it's worth it. Each interaction is a chance to build trust, deepen connections, and learn more about my own journey. Real listening is powerful. It changes us from the inside out, slowly breaking down the layers of ego that hold us back and opening us up to new levels of understanding. When we allow our ego to shift and adapt, we open ourselves up to grow alongside others.

Listening with self-awareness is an art—it's a skill that takes humility, patience, and a real openness to grow. The more I listen, the more I understand that my role isn't to fix people's problems; it's to create a space where they feel safe enough to find their own solutions. This isn't just about hearing what they're saying; it's about connecting with them, letting their words sink in, and reflecting on what those words mean for both of us. Every conversation reminds me of a simple truth: none of us is perfect, and that's completely okay.

Listening doesn't make me an authority or a problem-solver; it makes me a witness to someone else's truth. And really, that's enough. True listening is about being present, growing alongside others, and building a real connection. We don't have to have all the answers, nor should we try to play the role of someone's savior. We're here to share in the journey, to learn together, and to understand that we are, in the end, only human.

CHAPTER 04 | PARENTS WITHOUT EMPATHY

One of the most powerful tools any parent can use is empathy.

But what happens when empathy is missing? What happens when parents, under the pressures of life and the weight of expectations, begin to lose sight of their children's emotional world?

We have all been at some point where we felt that our parents didn't understand us, or we felt bitter about something they denied us because they couldn't comprehend why that thing mattered to us.

I get it: Parents—not every parent, though—want the best for their child. But at times, best might not be the right thing. And even if it is, it does more damage to a child emotionally than it does any good. And this happens mostly because parents sometimes do not think and see from the perspective of their children.

The problem? They lack empathy.

Parenting without empathy can create a disconnect, one that lingers far into adulthood. This chapter is about understanding that challenge, exploring the myth of the "perfect parent," and discovering how empathy can turn things around.

Many parents, knowingly or unknowingly, fall into the trap of control. They think they must be perfect, always right, and always in charge. But here's the truth: perfection isn't real, and control isn't connection. Parenting is not about having all the answers or fixing every problem. It's about walking beside your child, understanding their struggles, and feeling their pain as if it were your own. That's where empathy comes in. Empathy is the bridge—a tool that allows parents to connect with their children on a deeper, more meaningful level. And when you use it, it doesn't just improve your family relationships; it strengthens the entire community.

We'll also explore a tool, the "empathy screwdriver," which is a metaphor for turning things around with understanding, flexibility, and care. Finally, I'll share an emotional story to remind us of why empathy is not optional—it's essential.

The Pressures of Parenting and the Myth of Perfection

Every parent, at some point, feels the pressure to be perfect. The perfect provider, the perfect protector, the perfect leader. Society, family expectations, and even self-imposed beliefs can make parents feel like they need to control everything in their children's lives—what they do, how they behave, and who they become. And when things don't go as planned, frustration sets in. Parents might become stricter, demand more compliance, and stop listening to what their child really needs.

But the truth is, perfection is an illusion. No one gets it right all the time—and that's okay. Parenting isn't about being flawless; it's about being present. It's about being willing to learn and grow alongside your child.

This is where British psychoanalyst Donald Winnicott's concept of the "good enough mother" becomes so important.

Winnicott believed that parents don't need to be perfect to raise healthy, well-adjusted children. Instead, they only need to meet their children's basic emotional needs with consistency, care, and love. The "good enough mother" understands that making mistakes is part of parenting, and those mistakes can actually help children learn to cope with challenges. Children don't thrive because their parents are flawless; they thrive because their parents are present and emotionally available.

When parents try to be perfect, they often focus too much on controlling outcomes—what their child does, how they behave, or who they become. They may stop listening to their children's feelings or needs in their effort to "get it right." This can create a rigid environment where children feel pressured to meet impossible expectations. By contrast, the "good enough" approach allows for balance. It helps parents focus on what truly matters: connection, trust, and empathy.

Here's where empathy comes into play. Empathy asks you to pause and step into your child's shoes. It means asking, How do they see this situation? How do they feel? Am I listening to understand, or am I just enforcing my own agenda? A parent who embraces the "good enough" mindset doesn't expect perfection from themselves or their child. Instead, they aim to understand their child's emotions and help them navigate challenges with patience and care.

Many parents unknowingly trade connection for control. They focus so much on what their child should be doing that they forget to ask how their child is doing. When empathy is missing, communication breaks down. The child feels unheard, misunderstood, or even emotionally abandoned. Over time, this can create deep wounds that are hard to repair. Winnicott's ideas remind us that this disconnection isn't inevitable. By letting go of perfection and embracing the "good enough" philosophy, parents can build stronger, more supportive relationships with their children.

It's also important to recognize that the pressures of perfection often come from how parents themselves were raised. If they grew up in homes where control was emphasized and empathy was absent, they might unintentionally repeat those patterns. Winnicott's "good enough mother" offers a way to break this cycle. By focusing on being emotionally present rather than perfect, parents can create a new dynamic—one built on understanding and trust.

As Marshall Goldsmith puts it, What got you here may not get you there. What worked in 1950 or 1960 might not be effective in 2024. The tools of parenting must evolve. Today's parents are tasked with navigating a world that demands more flexibility, more listening, and more learning—especially from their children.

The good news is, it doesn't have to be this way. By letting go of the need to be perfect and embracing the "good enough" mindset, parents can shift their focus to what truly matters: being empathetic, supportive, and present. It's never too late to start creating deeper, more meaningful connections with your children.

The Empathy Screwdriver

The idea of the "empathy screwdriver" is simple yet powerful. Think about how a screwdriver works: it can tighten a screw or loosen it. It turns in both directions. The same concept applies to parenting with empathy.

Sometimes, a situation needs tightening—more structure, more clarity, or a little more effort to hold things together. Other times, it needs loosening—more flexibility, more patience, or a gentler approach to allow space for growth and understanding. A screwdriver gives you options, and empathy does too.

For example, imagine a parent asking a child to clean their room. If the child doesn't do it, the parent's instinct might be to raise their voice and enforce compliance. But what if the child doesn't know how to clean their room? What if they feel overwhelmed or unsure? An empathetic parent would stop and ask questions: *Do you understand what I'm asking you to do? Do you need help? Let's do it together so I can show you what I mean.*

By taking a moment to loosen the approach—to listen, to explain, and to connect—the parent empowers the child to succeed. Instead of frustration, the child feels supported. Instead of defiance, there's cooperation.

Sometimes, the empathy screwdriver also reveals when the tool itself needs to change. If a screw keeps falling out, maybe it's the wrong tool for the job. For parents, this means recognizing when one approach isn't working and being flexible enough to try something new. If communication is breaking down, it might be time to pause and reflect. Are you truly listening? Are you offering clear guidance? Empathy means looking at the problem together and finding solutions that work for everyone.

Seeing What You Might Miss

Parents often don't realize when their approach isn't working. There's a concept I like to call *reflective thinking*, which is about seeing something in yourself that you can't see on your own—like having dirt on your forehead. You don't know it's there until someone gently points it out.

For example, imagine you're frustrated because your child isn't listening. You keep repeating yourself, but nothing changes. A friend or mentor might step in and say, *Have you tried asking if they understand what you mean? Maybe they need you to explain it differently.* This small piece of feedback—someone holding up a "mirror"—can help you see where empathy might make all the difference.

Reflective thinking allows parents to ask themselves tough but necessary questions: *Am I truly listening? Am I considering my child's perspective? Is there something I'm missing here?* By being open to feedback and willing to adjust, parents can strengthen their connection with their children.

The Cost of Losing Empathy

There's a story that illustrates why empathy is so crucial in parenting. A mother, overwhelmed by life and trying to hold her family together, struggled to connect with her teenage son. He had become distant, withdrawn, and often angry. The mother, feeling helpless, believed the best approach was to enforce stricter rules and demand obedience. She stopped asking how he was feeling because she assumed he wouldn't tell her anyway.

One day, her son's anger turned to silence. He stopped coming out of his room, stopped talking, and stopped showing up for family meals. Weeks later, the mother found a letter he had written but never sent. In it, he expressed feelings of being unseen, unheard, and alone. He wrote, *"I don't think anyone cares how I feel."* Tragically, that mother never got the chance to repair their relationship. Her son's pain had gone unnoticed for too long, and the cost was irreversible.

This story is heartbreaking, but it's not uncommon. So many parents are so overwhelmed by their own challenges—work, finances, stress—that they lose touch with their children's emotional worlds. Without empathy, these cries for help can go unnoticed.

The lesson here is clear: empathy matters. Parents must be willing to pause, to listen, and to ask, *How is my child really doing?* It might feel awkward at first. It might even feel uncomfortable. But the alternative—losing that connection forever—is far worse.

Empathy: The Key to Relationships

At the heart of it all, empathy is the key to relationships. Whether you're a parent, a leader, a friend, or a partner, empathy is what allows you to connect with others on a deeper level. It's what allows you to understand their struggles, to feel their pain, and to walk beside them instead of ahead of them.

For parents, this means understanding that you are not God. You don't control everything. You don't have to have all the answers. And that's okay. Your role is not to be perfect but to be present. To listen. To care. And to be willing to learn alongside your child.

When parents lead with empathy, they create a foundation of trust and understanding. They show their children that it's okay to be imperfect. It's okay to struggle. And it's okay to ask for help.

Because at the end of the day, what children need most isn't a perfect parent. It's a parent who cares enough to understand them—who walks in their shoes, feels their pain, and helps them carry the load.

So remember this: You are not God; that job is already taken. What you *can* be, though, is the parent your child needs—empathetic, understanding, and present. That's the real key to building strong, lasting relationships with your children and creating a better future for your family and community.

CHAPTER 05 | ADDICTION & RECOVERY: LESSONS IN LETTING GO

Addiction is a battle that many don't even realize they are fighting. It's not a sudden war but a slow, creeping invasion, a quiet thief that sneaks in under the cover of routine and habit. It doesn't announce itself with sirens or flashing lights; it seeps in through the cracks, latching onto stress, loneliness, pain, and fear. It begins with small choices, little escapes—just one drink to relax, just one pill to take the edge off. But before you know it, those little escapes turn into something more, something that tightens its grip around your life and refuses to let go. It takes more than you ever expect: your health, your relationships, your identity.

The most deceptive part? The illusion of control.

Most people struggling with addiction don't wake up one morning and decide they're going to ruin their lives. They convince themselves that they're simply managing things their way. *I can stop whenever I want. It's just to take the edge off. I deserve this.*

These thoughts become a script, playing on repeat, convincing them that their choices are deliberate rather than dictated by dependence. But addiction is an expert liar. It lets you think you're in control even as it tightens its grip. It whispers to you, telling you that everything is fine, that you can handle it, that you're different from those who have lost everything. Until one day, you wake up and realize you've become exactly what you never thought you would.

The Reality of Addiction

One of the hardest parts of working in recovery is seeing how many people don't make it. I've attended more funerals than I care to count. I can still remember the first one: standing in a room full of grieving family and friends, feeling the heavy silence of what could have been.

I'm sure you, too, have experienced something like this at some point in your life, even if you're not an addict: a mother clutching a photo of her son, tears running down her face as she whispers, *"I just don't understand. He was doing so well."* Or a father standing off to the side, fists clenched, unable to say a word.

Every time I witness moments like these, I can't shake the thought of how unfair it is and how much potential is lost. Addiction doesn't care how deeply you're loved or how much hope surrounds you. Behind every loss, there's a story: a mother who never gave up, a father who held on to hope, a best friend who tried everything. The same cycle plays out again and again: desperate interventions, second, third, and fourth chances, love stretched to its breaking point. And still, sometimes, it's not enough.

Addiction is a disease of denial. It whispers that everything is fine even as things crumble. It convinces people they're functioning and that they can stop if they really want to. This is what makes intervention so difficult.

Many people struggling with addiction or using substances to self-medicate don't believe they have a problem. The challenge is helping them understand that they might, or that they do, and that they need to take action. Because addiction is a family disease, loved ones often try their hardest to help. But despite their best efforts, their actions can lead to unintended consequences, leaving them blaming themselves. Families recognize the sickness. They intervene. But the person struggling doesn't have the awareness to see it. Too often, this ends in tragedy, whether through self-inflicted harm or accidental overdose.

Meanwhile, the people who love them stand on the sidelines, watching the slow-motion wreckage, powerless to stop it. It's like watching someone drown, refusing to grab the life raft you're holding out. I've seen mothers call me sobbing, fathers asking if there's one more thing they can try, and siblings wondering if they should have said something different, done something more. And I tell them the same hard truth: you can't save someone who doesn't want to be saved.

That's the cruelest part of addiction: it doesn't just hurt the person using it. It drags everyone around them into the storm. Families suffer. Friendships fray. Relationships crumble. And sometimes, despite all the love and effort in the world, heartbreak is the only ending. Addiction is a tidal wave; it swallows everyone in its path, leaving only wreckage and unanswered questions.

My Own Battle with Addiction

Letting go of addiction isn't just about putting down the substance. It's about surrendering the need to control something that's already controlling you. And that? That's terrifying. I know because I've been there. I've seen it in my own life, and I've watched it play out in the lives of countless others, some who made it to the other side and some who didn't. I've watched people I cared about swear they would quit, only to fall back into the same cycle days later. I've seen the hope in their eyes turn to shame, the promises they made to themselves and their families shatter under the weight of withdrawal, cravings, and fear.

I don't like to spend too much time talking about myself, but I will say this—I've been there. I know the exhaustion of trying to outrun yourself, the relief of numbing, the justifications that keep you locked in the cycle. I know what it's like to look in the mirror and not recognize the person staring back at you. And I know how impossible it feels to admit that you need help. The shame can be suffocating. The fear of what life will look like without your crutch can feel unbearable. And yet, deep down, you know the path you're on only leads one way.

For me, I thought I was in control. Numbing myself allowed me to avoid rejection, failure, and even success—I didn't have to process feelings. But over time, my behavior started to shock and sadden those around me. People pointed out that I needed help. At first, I didn't see it, but eventually, I realized I had to make changes. Recovery didn't come to me in a single epiphany. It wasn't a dramatic moment of clarity but a series of small, painful realizations. It took time. It took breaking down and being willing to listen. It took learning to sit with discomfort instead of running from it.

When I finally let go, I understood that it's okay to not be okay. And it's also okay to be okay.

Yes, I've faced addiction myself. I got lucky. I survived, and I'm still surviving. My life's work is about helping others survive, too. The hardest part for me was accepting that I had this disease and that I needed help. I learned that sometimes, you have to seek expertise outside of yourself to get the right support. If you broke your leg, you wouldn't hesitate to see a doctor. If you had pneumonia, you wouldn't try to tough it out alone. But addiction convinces you that asking for help is a weakness. It isn't. It's survival. It's choosing life when everything inside you is telling you to give up.

The biggest lesson I learned? You don't have to do it alone.

Surrender

Many times, when someone is under the influence of a substance, they believe they're in control. They think self-medicating helps them manage their mind and emotions. What they don't realize is that they're actually losing control. When they're not using, they're forced to feel emotions like sadness, anxiety, and rejection. So, they go back to numbing themselves because it feels like a safe place. But the reality is, they're on a path that's destroying them. They don't see it that way. To them, they're just doing what they can with what they have to get through the day. That illusion of control is dangerous because it keeps them stuck in a cycle that's killing them.

Admitting you're not in control is one of the hardest things you'll ever do. People associate surrender with weakness, but it's the opposite. It takes incredible courage to say, "I can't do this alone." It takes strength to reach out for help. And it takes true humility to recognize that your way isn't working.

If someone reading this is struggling with addiction, I want them to take away one thing: there is always hope and help. But you have to be willing to take that first step. You don't have to keep living like this. You don't have to keep fighting alone. The moment you admit you need help is the moment you take back your power.

Addiction is like a compass that's just slightly off. At first, you don't notice. But over time, you find yourself miles away from where you are meant to be. The good news? There's always a way back. The road isn't easy, but it's there. And you don't have to walk it alone. There are hands reaching out to you, ready to pull you out of the dark. You just have to be willing to grab on.

So, no matter how far you've fallen, no matter how many mistakes you've made, you are not beyond saving. But you can't do it alone. And that's okay.

If you're reading this and you're struggling, reach out. The hardest step is the first one. But once you take it, you'll realize you were never truly alone. And you never have to be again.

CHAPTER 06 | EMBRACING IMPERFECTION

We're often told that if we just work harder, push further, and never slip up, we'll eventually reach this mythical place where everything is *perfect*.

Perfection…….

A word dreaded by many, I am sure, yet at the same time, worn proudly by some overworked, exhausted individuals who treat it like a medal, one they clutch tightly, even as it weighs them down. They chase it relentlessly, believing that once they achieve it, the emptiness will fade, the exhaustion will be worth it, and life will finally feel complete.

But perfection rarely offers relief unless it is truly driven by something intrinsic, shaped by your own values rather than external expectations. Otherwise, it only tightens its grip, demanding more with every step forward.

Society tells us we need to have it all together all the time. If we're not thriving in every area of life, we're failing. That's the message that's hammered into us from a young age. And for years, many of us buy into it.

But here's the truth: perfection is a moving target. It's an illusion. And the more you chase it, the more exhausted, anxious, and disconnected you become. It's a mirage in the desert, one that always seems just a little further ahead, making you run faster, push harder, never stopping to ask if the chase is even worth it. The pursuit of perfection isn't just unrealistic; it's more than that—it's dangerous. It keeps us stuck, makes us afraid to take risks, and convinces us that mistakes are something to be ashamed of instead of something to learn from.

And even if perfection did exist, it would never be a universal truth. What's perfect to you might be average to someone else. What someone else sees as ideal, you might see as lacking. There's no single definition, no finish line that everyone agrees on. The goalposts shift depending on culture, upbringing, personal values, and even trends. So, if perfection is entirely subjective, why do we wear ourselves down trying to reach a version of it that isn't even our own? Why do we exhaust ourselves chasing something that will never feel truly 'finished'? If you ever find yourself breaking under the weight of trying to be perfect, stop and ask: whose version of perfection are you even trying to achieve? And more importantly, is it making you happy—or just tired?

I used to believe that if I worked hard enough if I pushed myself just a little more, I could reach that elusive level of perfection. But over time, I realized something: perfection is unattainable, and more importantly, it's unnecessary. What's the point of reaching an impossible standard if it costs you your peace? What actually matters is progress: moving forward, even if it's messy. Growth happens through trial and error, not by getting everything right the first time.

So, let's talk about the pressure to be perfect, why it's so ingrained in us, and how we can start letting go of it. Because, at the end of the day, you are not here to perform for the world.

Where Does the Pressure Come From?

The pressure to be perfect isn't something we're born with. It's taught. It's reinforced through our families, schools, workplaces, and now, more than ever, social media.

In the workplace, there's a belief that you have to constantly prove yourself. But what exactly are we proving, and by whose standards? Who decides what 'excellence' looks like, and why do we all feel the need to measure ourselves against it?

Some people push themselves to overachieve, afraid that if they slow down for even a moment, they'll fall behind. Others do the bare minimum because they're terrified that excelling will set an expectation they can't maintain. Both extremes stem from the same fear: the fear of not being enough.

It's like those images you sometimes see on social media, where a group of animals, all from different species, are asked to climb the same wall. A fish, a monkey, an elephant, a bird. The test is the same, but their abilities are completely different. The fish isn't incompetent for not climbing; the elephant isn't failing for not soaring into the sky. Each excels in its own way, just not by the standard that was arbitrarily set for them. Yet, in our own lives, we don't stop to question whether the standards we're competing against even make sense. Instead, we just push ourselves harder, convinced that reaching the top, whatever that may look like, validates our worth.

And sadly, this sort of pursuit isn't limited to professional life only. In relationships, there's often an unspoken pressure to be the perfect partner—the one who never complains, never makes mistakes, never has a bad day. You're expected to always be understanding, always emotionally available, and always patient. But relationships aren't built on perfection; they're built on realness. When one person feels like they have to suppress their emotions to maintain peace or constantly perform as the "ideal" partner, the balance shifts. One person ends up carrying the emotional weight while the other coasts. Over time, resentment builds, and what started as love turns into obligation. You're no longer in a relationship; you're playing a role.

But real relationships aren't about being flawless; they're about being human together. They're about seeing someone at their worst and choosing to stay. They're about understanding that mistakes and bad days don't define love. How you work through them does.

Families have their own way of reinforcing perfectionism. Parents, often with good intentions, push their children to be better, to achieve more, and to never fail. But when failure is seen as unacceptable, kids grow up afraid to take risks. They don't see mistakes as learning experiences; they see them as proof that they're not good enough. The weight of perfection starts early, and unless we consciously challenge it, we carry it for life.

And when it comes to personal growth, the pressure to constantly improve can be overwhelming. We're told we need to be better versions of ourselves every day. But what happens when we hit a wall? When we can't keep up? Instead of allowing ourselves grace, we internalize the idea that we're not trying hard enough. We equate stagnation with failure, even when, sometimes, stillness is necessary for growth.

Perfectionism convinces us that we are only as good as our latest achievement. And that's a dangerous way to live. Because if your worth is always conditional, when do you get to just be?

My Own Struggles with Perfectionism

I know this struggle firsthand. Growing up, perfection was encouraged and *expected.* And sure, encouragement is great; it pushes you, helps you grow.

But expectations? Especially the kind that doesn't take into account who you are, what you're going through, or what actually matters to you? That's just a weight that drags you down. And that's exactly what happened to me.

If I wasn't striving to be the best, I was falling short. In my family, success wasn't about happiness or fulfillment. It was about achievements: straight A's, winning, and always one-upping the person next to you. If you weren't constantly perfecting yourself, then what were you even doing?

Growing up, that mindset followed me everywhere. In school, I pushed myself too hard, always comparing my grades to everyone else's. In my career, I worked longer hours than I should have, trying to prove myself over and over again. And when I failed, because failure happens, it felt like a disaster, not a lesson or a stepping stone.

For years, I believed that if I wasn't the best, I wasn't enough. But perfection is a trap. I wish I had learned it sooner. It never lets you rest or appreciate where you are. No matter what you accomplish, it whispers that it's not quite good enough. "Just a little more," it says. "Then you'll be okay." But the goalpost keeps moving.

Eventually, I hit a wall. I realized I couldn't keep chasing this impossible standard. More importantly, I didn't want to.

That's when it finally hit me. I wasn't failing at life. I was failing at being perfect. And honestly, that was the best realization I could have had.

The Social Media Effect

I have mixed feelings about this one. It's a marvel of technology, a force that has propelled the world forward faster than ever before. But at the same time, it feels like a demon with its claws sunk deep into people already struggling with their sense of self, their worth, and their direction in life.

Social media has taken perfectionism to an entirely new level. It's not just our immediate circles influencing us anymore. It's the whole world. Every day, we're bombarded with images of people who seem to have it all figured out.

The perfect body.

The perfect career.

The perfect relationship.

What once was a private struggle, comparing yourself to a handful of people in your school, your workplace, your neighborhood, has become a global phenomenon. Now, you're up against celebrities, influencers, and strangers with perfectly curated lives. You don't just compare your success to the people you know; you compare it to an entire internet filled with highlight reels. And it's an unfair fight.

But what we don't see is the reality behind the filter. We don't see the struggles, the self-doubt, the moments of failure. We only see the highlight reel. And when we compare our unedited, messy lives to someone else's curated perfection, we always come up short. Even if we logically know it's not real, the illusion still affects us. It still makes us question if we're enough.

Social media presents an exaggerated, often fabricated reality. It makes people believe they need to be thinner, richer, and more successful. And when they inevitably fail to reach these impossible standards, they feel worse than before. It's a cycle that fuels insecurity and anxiety.

But here's the truth: no one has it all together. No one is perfect. And the people who seem to be? They're just better at hiding their cracks.

What Happens When You Let Go of Perfection

The moment I let go of perfection was the moment I started living. I stopped measuring my worth by my achievements. I stopped holding myself to an impossible standard. I gave myself permission to make mistakes. And that's when everything changed.

Because here's the thing: when you're not afraid of failure, you take more chances. You grow. You learn. You stop worrying about what people think and start focusing on what actually matters. You shift from surviving to actually living.

Perfection is exhausting. Progress is freeing.

There is a clear and significant difference between both.

So, if you're someone who's struggling with perfectionism, ask yourself this: How's that working for you? Are you happy? Are you at peace? Or are you constantly chasing something that's just out of reach?

It's okay to want to do well. It's okay to strive for greatness. But perfection should never be the goal. Growth should be. Learning should be. Progress should be. And most importantly, peace should be.

At the end of the day, perfection is just one small mark in the sand. It's not the be-all, end-all. It's not the ultimate goal. It's just one possible destination. One of many.

If you spend your whole life chasing perfection, you'll miss out on everything that makes life real. The struggles. The mistakes. The messy, beautiful process of becoming.

So, instead of chasing something unattainable, focus on progress. Focus on learning. Focus on becoming the best version of yourself—not the perfect one.

CHAPTER 07 | HUMOR IS A MEASURING TAPE

There's something uniquely powerful about laughter. I am not talking about the kind that ignores pain or brushes over problems, but the kind that breaks the tension softens the moment, and says, "You're not alone."

For me, humor isn't just a way to lighten the mood—it's a measuring tape. It helps gauge where someone is emotionally. It reveals truths that might be too hard to say outright. And it gives people a way to breathe when the weight of life feels too heavy. In this chapter, I will talk about how humor shows up in my work, my life, and my philosophy. And before I get to that, I want to assure you that I DO NOT use it to hide from the hard stuff. In fact, just the opposite. Humor, for me, is often the first step toward healing.

I'm not exactly sure where the phrase *"humor is a measuring tape"* came from, but it stuck with me. And when I think about what it means to me, I'd say this: when someone brings humor into a moment, especially a tough one, it's a sign of honesty. It's really hard to be funny and fake at the same time. Humor, when it's real and respectful, usually carries a truth inside it. That's why I use it so often. It's part of who I am. It's not a strategy for me but something natural. It's how I show up, especially when someone's hurting or scared.

In those moments, humor helps me read the room. It lets me know how much someone can take in that moment. Are they shut down? Are they open? Are they ready to talk, or do they need a minute? A small laugh, just a crack in the wall, can tell me there's still some light getting in. That's the tape measure. That's how I know where we are and where we might be able to go next.

When I work with families, I often tell them, "It's not your fault." And they'll look at me and laugh, kind of nervously. One mom said, "How can it not be my fault? I'm the mother!" And I'll give an example, like—if your child eats too much and gets sick, that's not on you. And then we laugh. Even if we don't, it at least breaks the ice and eases our minds. It brings down the temperature so we can talk without everything being so charged. I use myself as an example, too, for the times I made a ridiculous decision or did something out of left field. I bring that into the space not to make light of serious things but to make people feel at ease. That's when real conversations happen.

It's tricky, though. Humor isn't always appropriate in a moment of crisis. It's delicate. But it can be helpful when the dust has settled. It can create a little distance between the person and their pain—not to disconnect them, but to give them room to breathe. I often say that humor is like the perfect water temperature in a bathtub. Or it's like a soft sweater that lets your guard down. It can help people feel safe enough to trust, to open up, to really connect. It doesn't replace the serious stuff. It just makes it easier to carry.

That little distance can be everything. When someone's overwhelmed, even a sliver of emotional space can help them reframe what they're going through. It doesn't change the facts, but it can change the way they sit with those facts. Humor can be that nudge from hopeless to hopeful, from frozen to fluid. I've seen people go from clenched fists to open hands in a single laugh. Not because their situation changed but because their outlook softened.

I've seen speakers and comedians do this beautifully. They talk about painful, real things, but they wrap it in humor. It helps people listen. It's like putting mustard and ketchup on a hot dog. It just helps it go down better. When someone's dealing with something overwhelming, a little laughter can be a pivot point. It's not a fix, but it can shift the energy.

Sometimes, people are so overwhelmed by life, so buried in pressure, they can't see a way out. I've said it before: pressure busts pipes. When that happens, humor can be the release valve. It's not about laughing at the crisis. Think of it more like refreshing our system, releasing some of the tension so we can think clearly again. I remember when I was going through my own personal trauma. I wasn't doing well. It was a dark time. Someone pointed it out to me in a really blunt, almost funny way, and I actually laughed. That moment didn't fix everything, but it cracked open a little space. It gave me hope.

Sometimes, the laugh comes first, and then the clarity. Sometimes, the moment of levity is what makes room for a deeper truth to land. I think of humor as a kind of guide. It walks people out of their cave. Not by dragging them, but by shining a little light and saying, "Hey, it's safe to come out now."

And there are lighter moments, too. Like when everything's falling apart, and I'll say, "Well, we're at the bottom—

nowhere to go but up." It's not always funny in the traditional sense, but it can change the tone, and let people exhale.

One story that sticks out is from when we were trying to open a Ben and Jerry's franchise. They had this program where nonprofits could run a shop. After a long visit, they told us no. They didn't think we served the population they were targeting. But we believed we did. So I told them, "I'd like to appeal your decision." They said, "We don't have an appeal process." And I just laughed and said, "Well, maybe we should start one." And to their credit, they laughed too. And they invited us to Vermont to make our case. We went, we shared our mission and our heart, and they reversed their decision. We opened the shop. And it became one of the most successful in their network.

That whole moment hinged on a laugh. A no turned into a yes, not because I argued harder, but because we connected as people. That's what humor can do—it creates a path. It shows you're human. It reminds everyone in the room that we're on the same side, trying to do good work.

Another time, we needed funding from the city for a housing project. My board members went to the city council on their own, and they were told no across the board. So I asked them, "Do any of you have another plan?" They didn't. I said, "Then let me try." I went back in, met with everyone I could, and laid out a new plan. I didn't want to embarrass anyone, but I believed in what we were doing. I brought a little lightness into those meetings, even though the stakes were high. And in the end, they reversed their decision, too. We got the funding, fixed the property, and served more people. It was a big win for the community.

That's what I mean when I say humor can move things forward. When people take themselves too seriously, they get stuck. They lose the ability to see the other side of the situation. They get locked into fear, or pride, or maybe even control. And when you're in that place, it's hard to hear anything else.

For me, one of the ways I break that cycle is by asking simple questions. Like, "How's that working for you?" If you're doing the same thing over and over and it's not getting you where you want to go, maybe it's time to try something new. That's when a little humor, just a nudge, can create a shift.

It's not about mocking. Not about sarcasm or cruelty. It's about timing. It's about knowing when a smile can make something softer, and when it's better to just sit quietly. Humor is a tool. But like any tool, it's only useful when used with care.

One of the funniest moments that still sticks with me is from my birthday party, either my 50th or 60th. My father-in-law had been drinking and stood up to make a toast. He said, "I want to introduce the birthday boy—the asshole who married my daughter." It was awkward, a little hurtful, but I turned it into a joke: "For my father-in-law, that's his way of saying 'I love you.'" And the whole room laughed. It took the edge off. Sometimes that's all humor needs to do.

And I see it in everyday conversations, too. A mother who lost her son introduced me to her mother, hoping I'd date her. I gently joked, "I'm flattered, but I am married." Years later, I shared that story with her daughter and we all had a good laugh. In grief, moments like that can be a lifeline.

I don't think you have to be a comedian to use humor. You just have to be open to it. Look for it. Practice it. Watch people who make others laugh and learn from them. Humor is like anything else. It can become a habit. And it's one of the few things in life that, when used kindly, rarely does harm.

I also believe that people who can laugh at themselves tend to be more grounded. They're usually more resilient, more real. They don't have to be perfect. They're okay being human. And after COVID, with all the isolation and stress, we need that kind of connection more than ever.

Humor is relational. It draws people together. It signals, "I see you, and I want to share this moment with you." When it's authentic, it builds trust. And trust, more than anything else, is what opens the door to change.

So if I had to sum this all up, I'd say this: it's okay to be not okay. We hear that a lot, but it's worth repeating because sometimes we forget. We try to power through, pretend we're fine, or push our feelings aside to keep things moving. But not being okay doesn't mean you're broken. It just means you're human.

And it's also okay to be okay, especially in situations where the world around you expects you to be falling apart. Sometimes, people feel guilty for finding peace, for laughing, or for taking a deep breath when others are still deep in the struggle. But beating yourself up doesn't help anyone. You don't have to prove your love by suffering endlessly. You don't have to write yourself into the ground just to show that you care. Sometimes, the most honest thing you can do is to stand in your calm and say, "This is where I am today. And that's okay."

And if humor helps, use it. Let it in. Share it. Laugh with others. Laugh at yourself sometimes. Don't be afraid to find light, even in the middle of the mess. Sometimes, it's those unexpected smiles that pull us through. A joke, a grin, or a well-timed one-liner can change the temperature of a room, shift the energy of a conversation, and remind people that joy and pain can exist side by side.

Because when things feel too serious, that's often the moment we need laughter the most. Not as a distraction but as a doorway. Laughter doesn't erase the pain. It just lets a little air in. It loosens the knot. It gives us the breath we need to keep going.

And if nothing else, remember this: it's really hard to be mad at someone who's smiling. Not because the smile fixes everything. But because it reminds us we're still connected. And connection, more than anything else, is what gets us through.

CHAPTER 08 | HOPE & HELP

So far in this book, I've talked a lot about control, specifically about letting go of it. In fact, that's pretty much the heart of this whole conversation. You might wonder why I keep stressing this point. Well, it's because once you truly accept that you can't control everything, your whole life opens up in unexpected, beautiful ways.

I've noticed something about us humans: we're incredibly hard on ourselves. We criticize ourselves so harshly that we forget we're just people. People with limits, people who can't possibly do everything right all the time. Accepting this reality doesn't mean you're giving up or that you failed. In fact, it might just mean you're brave enough to try a new way, maybe a better way. It can even make room for hope, for help, and for real peace.

It took me a long time, probably way too long, to realize how good it is that I'm not God. Seriously, imagine carrying all that responsibility. It doesn't make any sense for us humans to pretend we have everything figured out. When I say, "You're not God—that job is already taken," I mean you can stop acting like the weight of the whole world is yours to bear. You don't have to control everything, and honestly, you can't. Trying to will only make things worse, especially for you.

I've seen it happen again and again. Whenever someone tries to act like they have all the answers, it almost always goes wrong. Think about the times you've seen someone try to control a situation completely. There's no room left for anyone else. Teamwork falls apart, frustration builds, and instead of solving problems together, everyone ends up confused or angry. It stops being a team and turns into one person's dictatorship. And we all know dictatorships don't lead anywhere good.

Today, letting go of control feels harder than ever. People grip control tightly because they're scared or frustrated. Sometimes, it's because of ego or because deep down, they think they're smarter than everyone else. But here's the reality: when one person insists on being right all the time, everyone else steps away. Conversations stop, people withdraw, and the chance for real collaboration disappears. That kind of control might feel safe in the short term, but it ends up making things lonely and far more complicated.

I often wonder why it's so hard for people to ask for help. Is it pride? Is it fear? Maybe a little of both? Honestly, I think it usually comes down to ego. Nobody likes feeling weak or admitting they don't have it all together. A lot of people would rather struggle quietly than just say, "Hey, I need some help here." Sometimes they don't even realize they need help until someone else points it out. There's a reaction I like to call "the fuck everything and run" mindset. Instead of slowing down and asking for advice, people rush forward blindly, ignoring help until they crash.

The kind of help people avoid most often is emotional support, financial help, or just having someone who genuinely listens. When someone keeps making the same mistake without asking for help, things usually get worse, not better. Instead of reaching out, they might even become bullies, pushing others to accept their way of thinking. But bullying never helps. It only makes everyone feel powerless. Instead of real agreement, you're left with resentment, anger, and chaos.

I can think of a recent example from the news: a high-ranking government official (Secretary of Defense) repeatedly used unauthorized communication channels for sensitive information. When caught, instead of admitting their mistake, they blamed everyone else. This refusal to accept responsibility just creates confusion and distrust. We've seen it so many times, especially in politics. People refusing to own their mistakes and making things worse.

But even when things feel completely messed up, there's always hope. Hope means trusting that somehow, someway, the right thing will eventually happen. Hope helps you push through when life gets tough. It's believing there's a better path, even when you're stuck in a tight spot.

I've seen people face incredibly difficult moments. They felt beaten down, tired, and alone, but somehow they refused to quit. Their determination eventually opened new doors, new ideas, and new possibilities for themselves and for others too. Their strength became contagious, changing the way people around them thought. Sometimes, just holding on and pushing through can spark conversations that eventually change everything.

It's funny. We spend so much time beating ourselves up for making mistakes, as if we're supposed to be perfect. But being human literally means messing up sometimes. I've learned that when you admit your mistakes honestly, people respect you more, not less. It doesn't show weakness; it shows authenticity. It makes you real, relatable, and trustworthy.

I know personally that whenever I've messed up and admitted it openly, it's helped me grow. Apologizing isn't easy, but it always helps me become better. People around me see mistakes as normal human experiences, not permanent flaws. Actually, mistakes can bring people closer because they show vulnerability, honesty, and humility.

I truly believe our toughest struggles can turn into our greatest strengths. You've heard the saying, "No pain, no gain," right? Well, it's true. When we survive difficult experiences without getting bitter, we become stronger, kinder, and wiser. We become better leaders, better friends, and better examples. Our stories encourage others to face their own challenges bravely.

Helping others isn't just about being kind; it also helps the person giving the help. I've experienced the amazing power of sharing my own journey with people who feel hopeless. Sometimes, just seeing someone else overcome similar struggles is enough to inspire hope. It tells them they're not alone and gives them strength to keep going.

If you're reading this right now during a hard moment, please know this: there is hope. There is faith. If you're brave enough to look at yourself honestly, ask for help, and accept you're just human, something better is always possible. Even when life feels incredibly dark, that light you see at the end of the tunnel really is guiding you forward. It is not something to fear. So reach out, ask for help, and hold onto hope.

Doing life alone is incredibly hard. It's okay to need help, to ask for it, and to accept it. Someone once told me something beautiful: "We will love you until you can love yourself." And let me tell you, it really does make all the difference.

As I close this chapter, here's one simple truth I'd love you to hold onto:

"If you do what you've always done, you'll get what you've always gotten. But if you have hope and faith, anything is possible."

Always remember: it's okay not to be okay, and it's just as okay to be okay. Life isn't perfect, and neither are we. But with honesty, humility, and a little hope, we'll always find our way forward.

A NOTE BEFORE YOU GO….

If you've made it this far, let me start by saying thank you. Thank you for sticking with me through these pages. Thank you for showing up, for yourself most of all.

This isn't one of those books that pretends to have all the answers. I'm not trying to be a guru or some expert with a perfect plan. I'm just a guy who's been through some things, paid attention along the way, and wants to offer you what's helped me.

And if anything I've shared in this book lands with you, even just one line, then maybe that's the beginning of something good.

Personally, if there's one thing I hope has stayed with you through the pages of this book, it's this: you're not alone. Even when it feels like you are. This journey wasn't about preaching from a pedestal or handing out rules from a mountaintop. My sole purpose was to walk beside you, hand-in-hand, as someone who's stumbled, learned, asked for help, and kept trying.

That's it.

Nothing more. Nothing less.

This book is about real life. Messy. Unpredictable. Sometimes painful. But also full of moments that remind us we can grow, change, and even find peace, if we're willing to be honest with ourselves and open with others.

Let's slow down here together, one last time, and let me remind you that…

You don't have to have it all figured out…

No, you don't have to know everything before you begin. You are not supposed to have all the answers lined up before you take that first step. Where is the learning in that? The point is to take the risk and find the answers with all that you have, no matter how little. In the end, one thing is sure: that you will have more than what you began with, be it in terms of experience, knowledge, material gain, spiritual exploration, or whatever you might need ahead in your life.

There's nothing wrong with saying, *"I don't know what to do."* In fact, those five words can be some of the most freeing ones you'll ever say. Because they create space for help, for learning, for movement.

Second thing that I would like to remind you of is that **tools are useless if you don't use them.**

If you're going to fix a leak, you need a wrench. If you want to build a shelf, you'll need a hammer. And if you're trying to rebuild your life, or your mindset, or your relationships— guess what? You need tools for that too.

You've got some now. You've read stories. You've seen examples. You have read about failures too. So this book was definitely not a fairytale that you find hard to believe in. In fact, I believe (or at least hope) that you've probably nodded a few times thinking, "Yeah, that's me."

If I've got you there, I am glad. I am glad that you could relate to me. I am glad that I made you realize that you are not alone in this. And if I could be of help in helping you realize that, and you really want to know more from me, I would say, take it slow.

We're all being hit with information every day. Nonstop, loud, emotional, and often conflicting. Just because something's repeated doesn't mean it's true. That's why learning to pause is a tool in itself. Not everything has to be reacted to immediately. In fact, some of the best decisions I've ever made came after I waited, listened, and sat with the discomfort for a little while.

Think of it this way: wisdom often speaks in whispers, not in noise. So give yourself the silence to hear it.

Then the real questions come: will you use what you've gathered?

I've never once regretted using these tools. What I have regretted is trying to do it all myself, and wearing myself out in the process.

So take inventory. Dust off your old tools. Try new ones. Borrow a few from someone else's toolbox until you build your own. That's how you grow.

And the last thing, ***aim for progress, not perfection.***

You want to make a change? Cook a new dish? Run a marathon? Build a relationship? You're going to screw up at first. That's okay. Don't let perfection be the enemy of progress.

In fact, *fail frequently so you can succeed sooner.* If you're afraid of looking foolish, try anyway. If you're scared to try again, do it gently. But don't stop. Give yourself permission to get it wrong. And keep going.

We all screw up. We all fall short. Sometimes we shoot the arrow and miss the target entirely. That doesn't mean you're broken. It means you're trying. And trying matters more than getting it perfect the first time.

You'll get better with practice. You'll feel more at ease. And slowly, your fear, your guilt, your frustration? They'll lose their grip on you.

It takes time. Be patient with yourself. Be kind. Give yourself permission to take a left turn instead of always making that same right. Try something new. Look around. Ask questions. Talk to someone who might know a little more than you do.

That's how we get better. That's how we move forward.

So, we are almost at the end of this book. You've got the knowledge now. You've read the stories. You've gathered the tools.

Now I'm asking you to do something simple, but powerful: make the 12-inch journey from your head to your heart. Let what you've learned become how you live. Not all at once, not perfectly, but intentionally.

Because that's where real change lives.

Not in the facts. Not in the quotes. But in the quiet decision to take one small action that lines up with who you're becoming.

And as for ***"You're Not God. That Job's Taken..."*** That isn't just a catchy title. It's a reminder. You're not supposed to control everything. You never were. And that's not a bad thing. That's freedom.

That's the whole heart behind this book.

I don't think of it as a religious thing. It's a spiritual anchor for me. A reset. A way to stop, breathe, and remember what really matters.

And if life ever feels overwhelming, I offer you the same tools I've used almost every day for forty years.

They helped me when I was stuck. They helped me when I was excited and wanted to move too fast. They helped me when my wife told me not to write another book... and I had a new idea the next morning.

So, I leave you with these tools, and a prayer. And the invitation to find your own version of peace, clarity, and acceptance.

This book will help you UNF**K yourself.

– Scott H. Silverman

THE SERENITY PRAYER

God, grant me the serenity

to accept the things I cannot change,

courage to change the things I can,

and wisdom to know the difference.

Got thoughts, questions, or need support? I'd love to hear from you — visit www.yourcrisiscoach.com to reach out.